Bicycle Blues

by

Anthony Masters

Illustrated by Harriet Buckley

First published in Great Britain by Barrington Stoke Ltd
10 Belford Terrace, Edinburgh EH4 3DQ
Copyright © 2000 Anthony Masters
Illustrations © Harriet Buckley
The moral right of the author has been asserted in
accordance with the Copyright, Designs and
Patents Act 1988
ISBN 1-902260-66-X
Printed by Polestar AUP Aberdeen Ltd

MEET THE AUTHOR - ANTHONY MASTERS

What is your favourite animal?
My bantams
What is your favourite boy's name?
David
What is your favourite girl's name?
Penny
What is your favourite food?
Chinese food
What is your favourite music?
Mexican
What is your favourite hobby?
Canoeing

MEET THE ILLUSTRATOR - HARRIET BUCKLEY

What is your favourite animal?
A cat
What is your favourite boy's name?
Ernest
What is your favourite girl's name?
Emily
What is your favourite food?
Spinach
What is your favourite music?
'There She Goes' by The La's
What is your favourite hobby?
Playing the harmonica

Barrington Stoke was a famous and much-loved story-teller. He travelled from village to village carrying a lantern to light his way. He arrived as it grew dark and when the young boys and girls of the village saw the glow of his lantern, they hurried to the central meeting place. They were full of excitement and expectation, for his stories were always wonderful.

Then Barrington Stoke set down his lantern. In the flickering light the listeners were enthralled by his tales of adventure, horror and mystery. He knew exactly what they liked best and he loved telling a good story. And another. And then another. When the lantern burned low and dawn was nearly breaking, he slipped away. He was gone by morning, only to appear the next day in some other village to tell the next story.

Contents

Chapter 1
The Stolen Bike

Jamie felt a cold shiver run through him. His brand new mountain bike was no longer padlocked to the lamp post. Someone must have stolen it while he was in the corner shop buying a cold drink.

Jamie always used the padlock Dad had given him years ago. So what could have gone so horribly wrong? Then Jamie saw something glinting in the gutter. It was his padlock and chain.

He bent down and picked them up and shoved the chain in his pocket. The padlock was open and when he tried to snap it shut the catch didn't work. Jamie stared sadly at the padlock. It was not surprising that it didn't work. Rust had been eating away the catch for years.

Jamie blamed himself completely. It was just after lunch on a hot Saturday in July and the streets were deserted, but someone must have seen him lock his bike and then discovered that the padlock was useless.

Jamie knew he should have bought a new padlock. There had been a number of mountain bike thefts on the estate this year, so why hadn't he been more careful? He was filled with rage. If he found out who the thief was, he knew what he'd do to him!

Jamie was tough and streetwise. He was also the natural leader of a group of boys at school whose main interest was playing in the local football league.

But how was he going to find the thief? Jamie knew that was going to be very difficult indeed and he didn't even know where to start.

He gazed around the central square of the estate. The streets went off in all directions and he could see dust rising in the summer haze. Jamie was sweating badly. What were his parents going to say? They'd saved up for his new bike for a long time. It had been his birthday present. Dad and Mum would be furious.

Then Jamie saw Bernie Harris leaning against the wall by the fountain that no longer worked and was full of rubbish instead.

Bernie was in a gang that hung out on the estate. They were into football too, but

had just been beaten by Jamie's team in the league. Had they wanted to have a go at him because of that? Like steal his bike?

Trying to look cool, Jamie strolled over to Bernie.

"What do you want?" Bernie sounded uneasy.

"Someone has nicked my bike. Did you see anyone?"

"I've only just got here."

"You didn't see me go into the shop?"

"No."

"Or come out?"

"I've only just got here," repeated Bernie. "Didn't you use a padlock?"

"Yeah."

"So how did your bike get nicked?"

"Dunno."

"Is that the padlock?" Bernie was gazing at him with a sarcastic grin on his face. "That rusty, old thing? Let's have a look."

"No chance."

"That couldn't padlock a packet of cornflakes." Bernie's grin widened.

Jamie turned away, feeling an idiot.

"Where are you going?" asked Bernie.

"To fetch my old bike."

"No need to padlock that old wreck," Bernie sneered.

"I'm going to take a ride round," Jamie yelled over his shoulder. "I'm going to find my new bike. And when I find who's taken it ... "

"No chance," said Bernie. "There's a gang operating round here."

Jamie turned round and walked back to Bernie with his fists clenched. "You know something about this, don't you? Where's my new bike?"

"Haven't a clue." Bernie leapt off the wall as Jamie got nearer.

"Who's got it?"

"How should I know?" Bernie broke into a run. "You shouldn't have been so stupid. Fancy having a rusty padlock that doesn't work!"

Jamie felt more angry than ever. He was sure that Bernie knew something. But if he laid a finger on him, Jamie was certain

Bernie's brothers would do him over. There was no point in setting up even more trouble for himself.

Chapter 2
The Search

As he ran home, Jamie's rage reached boiling point, but the rage was largely directed against himself. How could he have been so stupid as to go on using that rusty, old padlock? Why hadn't he saved up and got a new one? Bernie was right.

Then Jamie began to wonder if Bernie had been the look-out for the gang. Had he hung around afterwards on purpose just to see Jamie's reaction? Was he even now running back to the gang to tell them? He could imagine them all having a good laugh at his expense.

Seeing an old bucket in the gutter Jamie aimed a kick at it and then howled with pain. He realised too late that the bucket was filled with hardened cement.

When he got home, Jamie was in such a temper that he couldn't stop himself punching the garage door. Not once but twice. As a result, his knuckles hurt badly. Luckily his parents were both out shopping.

He dragged out his old wreck of a bike and cycled back through the hot streets, determined to search the estate. Sweat poured down Jamie's face and his mouth was dry, but he never even thought of getting another drink. He had to find his mountain bike.

The streets of the estate were busier now and there were crowds of kids hanging around in the square, while others were on the playing field, kicking a ball about.

Jamie knew some of the kids so he waved at them. Others he didn't know at all and they were the ones who seemed to look shifty. Were they whispering about him behind his back? Did they know where his bike was?

There was no sign of Bernie, but Dean Parsons cycled past him. He was grinning. Why? wondered Jamie.

Dean was a couple of years younger than Jamie and wasn't a member of the gang. But his brother was. Did Dean know something?

"Oi!" yelled Jamie.

Dean came to a halt with a shriek of brakes. "What do you want, then?"

"What are you grinning at?" Jamie demanded.

"Not a lot."

"You seen my new bike?"

"What new bike?" There was still a faint grin on Dean's face.

"The one I got given for my birthday."

"Didn't know you had a birthday – *or* a new bike." Dean began to cycle away.

Jamie would have chased him but he knew his old wreck didn't have the speed. His temper rose. Again.

Jamie rode the streets for over an hour in the boiling summer heat, but he was beginning to realise his search was hopeless. Had Dad remembered to insure his mountain bike? Would he get the money back so he could buy a new one? After all, the insurance people might refuse to pay up because his padlock had rusted away. Jamie was sure that one way or another they wouldn't pay out the money. He was filled with despair.

Then just as he was heading down a quiet side street he saw an amazing sight.

His brand-new, gleaming mountain bike was leaning up against a garden wall. He just couldn't believe his own eyes.

Was someone playing a joke? Or had the thief only taken his mountain bike for a joy ride and then dumped it?

Whatever had happened, Jamie was overjoyed. He also knew he had to act fast.

No one was around and he jumped off his old wreck, his heart pounding. He carefully leant it against the wall and then ran towards his new mountain bike. There wasn't a scratch or a dent. It was as beautiful as ever and Jamie couldn't believe his luck.

He grabbed the bike and rode off. Never had he been so happy.

Jamie glanced back but there was still no one around. He felt a sudden twinge of regret. Jamie had loved his old wreck. He couldn't just leave it propped up against a wall.

Then Jamie had an idea. He'd explain to Dad what had happened and they'd come back and collect the old wreck in the car.

Chapter 3
The Wrong Bike

Jamie was halfway home when he noticed something. There was a pattern of purple stars along the crossbar of this bike and a purple bird on the top of the mudguard.

He skidded to a halt.

Jamie got off and gazed down carefully at the crossbar. Didn't his bike have dark

blue stars? And wasn't his bird dark blue too?

He broke out into a sweat. This couldn't be happening – but it was. This mountain bike wasn't *his* mountain bike. It was someone else's.

The colour of the markings was only slightly different – but different all the same. In his excitement he'd taken the wrong bike. In fact, he had just stolen a mountain bike!

The disappointment was awful. But with the disappointment came fear. He could get nicked for this. No one would believe that he had taken the wrong bike by accident. So what was he going to do?

Jamie had never been so scared.

Then Bernie rode up. Could he have been following him?

"So you got it back, then?" Bernie said, staring at Jamie.

What kind of look was that? Jamie wondered. "Er … yes."

"You don't sound very sure. Is it OK?"

"What?"

"Has the bike been damaged?"

"No."

"Then why are you staring at it in that weird way?"

"Just checking." Jamie felt more and more guilty. But why should he? He'd made a mistake. A mistake anyone could make. Or was it?

"Where did you find your bike?" asked Bernie. He seemed completely bewildered and more than a little scared himself.

"On the other side."

"Other side of what?"

"The estate." Jamie was getting flustered now.

"Where *was* it?" Bernie was getting impatient.

"Leaning against a wall."

"What wall?"

"I dunno." Jamie was feeling more and more uncomfortable.

"You just took it?"

"You bet I did."

"And rode the bike away?"

"I wasn't going to push it, was I?" said Jamie scornfully.

"So you don't know who took it?"

"I don't need to. I've got the bike back, haven't I?"

"You don't sound very pleased." Bernie was still looking at him strangely.

"It was a shock."

Bernie yawned too casually. Jamie noticed that he was sweating too. Was it just the heat, or was he afraid of something?

"Better be getting on. I want my dinner." Bernie cycled away.

Jamie felt more and more uneasy. He jumped on the mountain bike and began to cycle back the way he had come.

Jamie glanced down at his watch. So far he'd been away for half an hour. Maybe the owner wouldn't have noticed his bike had gone.

Could he get it back and ride away on his old wreck without anyone knowing what had happened?

Jamie began to feel more hopeful. But then he remembered that his brand-new mountain bike was still missing and felt a lump of misery that seemed to turn to ice in his stomach.

Chapter 4
Greg

When Jamie pedalled into the quiet side street he saw to his relief that his old wreck was still propped up against the garden wall.

Jamie quickly jumped off the mountain bike and propped it against the wall. He was trembling with fear.

Could he get away with it? He *had* to.

Running back towards his old wreck he grabbed the bike by the handlebars and was just about to leap on when a voice yelled, "Oi! You!"

Jamie gazed down the garden path to see a boy he knew from school running towards him. It was Greg Dawson. Worse still, Greg was a member of the team they had beaten at football last week.

Jamie grabbed his old bike and jumped on. He got the timing wrong and almost fell off. Then he steadied himself, wobbled and steadied himself again.

By this time the boy was within a metre of him. Then he grabbed hold of Jamie's handlebars. "Jamie!" he yelled. "You're a thief! I'm going to fix you for this."

Greg began to shake Jamie's bike hard. Jamie tried to push him away but Greg was too strong and finally Jamie fell off, landing on the ground with a thump.

"I can explain," he gasped.

"How?"

"It was the wrong bike." Jamie scrambled to his feet, noticing that Greg was already bunching his fists.

"What do you mean?" shouted Greg. "Isn't my new mountain bike good enough for you? It was a present for working hard at school. Now I'm going to work hard on you. I'm going to beat you to a pulp. I'm going to ..."

"Just let me explain."

"There's nothing *to* explain." Greg was coming nearer, fists still clenched, the muscles in his arms bulging.

"You've got to listen."

"I'll give you ten seconds to give me a good reason for not beating you up. And I warn you, I'm not going to believe anything you say."

"I had *my* mountain bike stolen," yelled Jamie, talking fast, so fast Greg could hardly understand what he was saying. "So I got my old wreck out …"

"Your what?"

"This old wreck out and started to search for the new mountain bike Dad gave me for my birthday. The one that got nicked."

"And took mine instead." Greg was staring at him. He looked bewildered, as if he was confused and could not understand what was going on.

"I thought it was *mine*!" continued Jamie, sure that Greg would never, ever believe him and he'd end up in court.

Greg hesitated, gazing at him as if he was trying to work out a difficult problem. "No two bikes are the same."

"I only realised that when I took a careful look." Jamie glanced at Greg and saw how puzzled he was. Suddenly Jamie wondered if he was in with a chance. He began to talk more slowly, trying to calm down and convince Greg that he'd made an honest mistake. "The two bikes are almost the same, but yours has got a purple bird on the mudguard and I've got a dark blue one. Your bike's got purple stars and mine's got dark blue. As soon as I discovered the mistake I rode your bike back here." He paused. "Hadn't you noticed it was gone?"

"I was inside doing my homework," Greg snapped.

"So you only saw me when I rode up."

"Dead right I did and you'd be dead if ..."

"If what?"

"If I didn't believe you."

"*What?*" Jamie stared at him in amazement.

"You heard."

"So you *do* believe me?"

"The story's so weird it's got to be true." Greg unclenched his fists and stepped back.

They continued to stare at each other.

"A lot of bikes have been nicked from round here over the last few weeks," said Greg. He paused for a moment. "And I reckon I have an idea where those bikes might be."

Jamie gazed at him, too shocked to really take in what Greg was saying. "Why don't I help you find your bike?"

"What?"

"Why don't I help you find your bike?"

"How can you?" asked Jamie hopelessly.

"I saw Mick Mason hanging round the closed-down garage in Tenby Drive the other day. I just wonder if he might be hiding stolen bikes in there."

Jamie still felt too shocked to be hopeful. "Wouldn't the police have checked the place?"

"Maybe, but Mick's clever. He could have found a really good hiding place in that old garage. It's been closed for years."

Jamie stared at Greg with distrust. Why

was he being so helpful? Could he trust him? Or was Greg setting up a trap in revenge for having his bike taken? On top of all that Greg belonged to the football side that Jamie's team had beaten. But he knew he didn't have any choice. Jamie was desperate to get his bike back.

"I'll give it a swing," he muttered in a weak voice.

"I'll lock up the bikes. I was an idiot leaving mine outside like that – *and* when I knew about all those thefts."

"So why did you?" Jamie was still very suspicious.

Greg went red. "There was something on TV I wanted to watch before I did my homework and I was late for the start of the programme. So how come yours got nicked?"

"I had this old padlock that didn't work."

"So you're a complete idiot too," Greg replied.

After they'd locked up their bikes in Greg's garage, the two boys set out on foot. The sun was still blindingly hot.

Greg and Jamie walked on for about ten minutes until they came to a part of the estate that was poor and run-down. Most of the houses and shops were boarded up and a few old cars had been dumped in a small park. Some of the cars had been set on fire and were burnt-out. Next to the park was the closed-down garage, a big shed-like building with an iron roof and broken windows.

Jamie gazed about him, feeling unsafe and unsure. Could he really trust Greg? Or was Greg just enjoying winding him up? So when was the trap going to be sprung? Was

Greg going to lock him in the garage as a punishment for taking his bike? Or had he planned something even worse?

"This is where I saw Mick Mason shoving something through a broken window," said Greg.

"Which one?" asked Jamie.

"Round the side."

"Why didn't you do something?"

"Wasn't my business, was it?"

"So it's your business now?" Jamie was even more suspicious.

"I don't like Mick. No one does. He's a bully. A lot of people would like to see the guy nicked and put away for a good, long time."

"Did Mick see you when he was pushing stuff through the window?"

"I'm not sure. I was just going for a bike ride."

Jamie knew he had to be satisfied with that explanation – except that he wasn't satisfied at all. He was sure he was being led into a trap.

Chapter 5
The Closed-Up Garage

"What are we going to do?" asked Jamie nervously.

"Try and get in."

"Someone will see us."

"That's a chance we've got to take."

Looking round to make sure no one was watching, they ran to the side of the old

garage. The broken window was quite large.

"Come on," said Greg. "We've got to check the place out."

Jamie hesitated. Then he thought of his brand-new mountain bike. He *had* to get it back. He decided to take the risk.

"Who's going in first?"

"I will," said Greg.

Jamie wondered if this was a good idea. But Greg was already scrambling over the sill, checking that he hadn't been spotted. He then climbed through the window and dropped down into the darkness inside.

"Are you coming or not?" Greg whispered. He wanted to get going.

Jamie also checked to see if anyone was around. Then he, too, climbed up on to the sill, got through the window and jumped down into the darkness.

"Where are you, Greg?" he hissed.

"Just over here."

But Jamie couldn't see anything or anyone. He was standing on a hard, concrete floor. Jamie could smell oil and petrol and a musty emptiness. "Why didn't we bring a torch?" he whispered.

"Didn't think of it," said Greg.

They stood there, not knowing what to do next. Jamie hoped his eyes would get used to the dark, but all he could see were dim, shifting shadows.

Then they both caught sight of a pool of light.

"Let's go over there," said Jamie. "We'll be able to see better."

They picked their way carefully over the oily, slippery floor. They were relieved to be standing in the light. Now Greg and Jamie could see the shadowy workshop a little more clearly.

The space was large and square with a couple of inspection pits. Jamie knew they were lucky not to have fallen into them. One of the pits was covered over but the other was wide open. Greg pulled aside the metal cover but neither of them could see anything in the pit below. Suddenly there was a scampering sound and they both froze.

"What's that?" gasped Greg.

Something large and dark and furry ran over Jamie's foot and he cried out, the fear moving coldly inside him.

"That was a rat," he hissed, shivering. "Let's get out of here." Jamie didn't think he could bear to stay in this awful place a minute longer.

He glanced at Greg, feeling ashamed of himself, but Jamie saw Greg looked as scared as he was. They were in this together.

"Wait a minute," said Greg. "What's that over there?"

In the dim light Jamie could only see a faint outline of a door on the opposite wall. Slowly and carefully, they both moved over to the door, only to find that it was locked. Jamie began to rattle at it – and then began kicking it.

"Don't make such a row," Greg warned him. "Someone will call the police. Or, worse still, Mick and his gang might turn up."

Jamie stopped rattling and kicking, and stood in front of the door breathing hard. "It's locked," he muttered. Then Jamie saw something that surprised him. "Wait a minute."

"What is it?"

"This lock's new. That's a bit weird, isn't it? A new lock in a garage that's not used any more."

"So what are we going to do?" asked Greg. He seemed to have lost his nerve and was shaking all over.

"Let's break the door open."

"We could be in trouble." Greg sounded as if he was on the edge of panic. "The police could have us for damaging property."

"We're in enough trouble already," said Jamie firmly. "Like trespassing. So we might just as well do a bit of breaking and entering."

Jamie slammed his shoulder into the door. The thump was hard and painful, but he felt something move. He tried again but this time the door felt more solid.

"Let me try," said Greg. He moved back, took a long run and gave a howl of agony as his shoulder made contact. But the door suddenly sprang open with a crunching sound, sending Greg into the darkness beyond.

"You OK?" asked Jamie.

"No," mumbled Greg. "I'm not. I'm in pain."

Jamie joined Greg in an even darker space. Again they could barely see, but after a while Jamie realised they were looking at a number of familiar shapes, all jammed together.

Bikes.

"I was right," whispered Greg.

Jamie nodded. He grabbed the handlebars of one of the bikes, making a crashing sound.

"Keep it quiet," hissed Greg.

"Maybe this is mine." Jamie pulled again and the bike suddenly came free.

He wheeled the bike over to the patch of light. "It *is* mine!" he yelled. "It's my new mountain bike."

"Shut *up.*" Greg was terrified. "You've got to stop shouting."

"OK," Jamie whispered. "OK. But I'm sure it's my bike." He checked carefully, not wanting to make a mistake a second time round. At last he was satisfied. "I know it's mine," he told Greg.

"So what are we going to do now?"

"Go to the police."

"You'd better leave your bike here then. It's evidence."

"I'm not leaving this bike anywhere again – at least, not without a padlock that works," snapped Jamie. "There's plenty of other bikes still there if it's evidence they want."

"OK." Greg seemed to be getting some confidence back. "Let's get your bike out of the window. But we'll have to be careful. If anyone sees us we could get mistaken for the gang."

"Thanks," said Jamie. "You've been terrific." He paused. "I didn't trust you at first. I thought you might be winding me up or leading me into a trap or something. But I trust you now."

Greg nodded. "All I want to do is to get out of here fast ... and I mean fast."

"OK. We'll get my bike out of the window. You go home. I'll cycle to the police station – it's only down Neville Avenue. Then we'll meet up again."

Greg looked doubtful. Then he said quickly, "All right then, but we've got to be really careful."

Jamie wheeled his precious bike to the window.

"I'll climb back outside and you pass it through to me," said Greg. "And make it snappy."

Once Greg was standing on the ground outside, Jamie pushed the front wheel and handlebars through the window and then stood on tiptoe, trying to push the rest of his bike through. But the more he struggled the more the frame kept jamming.

"Help me!" yelled Jamie.

"Shut up!" hissed Greg.

"Are you going to help me or not?"

"I'm trying to. Keep your voice down."

"Nothing's happening." Jamie was getting angry and frustrated.

"I'm pulling the handlebars. What else can I do? One of the pedals must be stuck." Greg sounded as if he was in a mega-panic again.

"Unstick it then!"

"I can't."

Suddenly the bike seemed to free itself. It hurtled through the window, the back mudguard catching Jamie's finger. From the howl of pain outside another part of the bike must have hit Greg.

As Jamie scrambled through, he saw Greg lying on the ground with the mountain bike on top of him.

"Be careful," Jamie yelled. "Don't damage my bike."

"I'll damage you in a minute," growled Greg as he got to his feet, looking round in a panic to see if they'd been observed. Luckily there seemed to be no one around.

"That's a smart mountain bike," came a familiar voice. "Now I wonder where you found that?"

Chapter 6
The Gang

Bernie was strolling towards them, a nasty grin on his face. With him was a tall skinhead with tattoos on his arms. He looks really heavy, thought Jamie. But oddly, instead of being afraid, Jamie just felt numb.

"Mick Mason," whispered Greg. "Now we're in real trouble."

"What are you doing here?" Jamie asked,

the numbness disappearing, only to be replaced by a creepy, cold feeling.

"Minding my own business. Doesn't look as if you're doing the same, does it?" Bernie demanded, the familiar, mocking grin on his face.

"Doing a bit of breaking and entering?" teased Mick.

"I was rescuing my bike." Jamie was indignant.

"What are you doing here, Mick?" asked Greg uneasily.

Mick didn't reply.

"You *sure* that's your bike?" said Bernie. "Thought yours had purple stars."

After all that had happened Jamie had a sudden twinge of doubt. He looked down and checked again. Of course it was his bike. "Don't be stupid," he said, stammering slightly.

Mick turned to Greg. "Who's your friend?" he asked and there was menace in his voice.

"None of your business," snapped Greg.

"My mates might think it *is* my business." Mick sounded even more menacing as some other young thugs appeared from round the back of the garage.

Jamie knew that neither he nor Greg would stand a chance against this lot.

"Nice to have a rich Daddy," said Mick, looking at Jamie's bike.

"My Dad saved up to buy this."

"Did he now?"

"And you stole it," yelled Jamie, suddenly losing his cool.

"That's a nasty thing to say." Mick was threatening Jamie and Greg as his gang came closer.

"We've got to make a run for it," hissed Jamie.

"I'm ready when you are."

"Let's go!"

Jamie rode his mountain bike hard at the half circle of thugs. He felt a hand grab his shoulder and someone else kicked out at his mudguard – but the kick didn't connect.

Glancing back he saw that Greg was running in the opposite direction, pursued by four members of the gang. But he seemed to have got off to a good start and they were already having trouble keeping up with him.

Then Jamie noticed that Mick had grabbed his own bike from behind the garage. So had another of his mates and they were pedalling after him at full speed.

Bernie had also joined the chase but Jamie knew that he could easily outpedal him. He wasn't so sure about Mick and his mate. They were cycling really fast.

"We've got to get him, Darren," yelled Mick.

Jamie was strong and fit, but when he looked back he was alarmed to see that Mick and Darren were much nearer.

Then Jamie made a fatal mistake. He had meant to go down Neville Avenue towards the police station. By accident, he made a wrong turn into a road that led to some high-rise flats – all of which were empty and waiting to be pulled down.

The surface of the road was bumpy and all kinds of junk had been dumped, making it like an obstacle course. Jamie skidded round an old safe, a couple of bike frames without wheels, some dustbins, a freezer unit and what looked like part of a caravan.

Every time he slowed up, Mick and Darren got nearer. Glancing over his shoulder and not looking where he was going, Jamie hit what was left of an armchair.

He fell off his bike and bounced over the chair, the sharp, exposed springs cutting his arm. Jamie rolled over and struggled to his feet. Then he saw that Mick had also hit the chair and was caught up in the springs, kicking out and swearing. Darren hurried over to help him and, seizing his chance, Jamie ran for his bike.

"Get him!" yelled Mick.

Jamie had just climbed on to his bike when Darren grabbed at him and he fell off again, the bike crashing to the hard tarmac. He stood up and charged at Darren, all his rage returning as he wondered if his bike had been damaged. Swinging his fist he caught Darren full in the face and blood spurted from his nose. Then Jamie kneed him in the stomach and he went down, gasping with pain.

Mick kicked out again at the chair springs, but the more he struggled the more the springs coiled around his boot.

Jamie leapt back on his bike, riding away as fast as he could, heading for the police station. His new mountain bike sped along and there seemed to be no sign of any damage.

When he looked back, he saw that Darren had managed to get to his feet while Mick had kicked himself clear of the springs. Jamie knew they would soon be after him. He began to pedal even faster, using the gears as much as he could, knowing he hadn't a moment to lose.

Chapter 7
Saving Greg

Gasping for breath and sweating more than ever, Jamie wheeled his bike into the police station. He was determined not to leave it outside only to be stolen again. But when the Sergeant behind the desk saw the bike he shouted, "You can get that out of here for a start!"

"It's evidence."

"What of?"

"Someone nicked this bike of mine."
Jamie was getting very worked up.

"How come you got it back?"

"I'll tell you ..."

"Not with that dirty bike in here you
won't. Shove it outside."

"I haven't got a padlock."

"So that's how your bike got nicked in
the first place?"

Jamie looked shamefaced. "I did have a
padlock."

"So?"

"It didn't work."

"That's what I mean. You kids should always ..."

"Look," said Jamie in despair. "My mate's being chased by a gang of bike thieves. You've got to do something."

"How do you know they're thieves?"

"Because they've got all the stolen bikes stashed away in that old garage in Tenby Drive."

"How do you know that? Did you break in?"

"We had to. I found my bike there – and loads of others."

"You should have left your bike where it was."

That was just what Greg had warned him about. "You've got to *do* something," he said urgently. "They could have beaten up my mate by now."

At last the Sergeant seemed satisfied. "All right, son. Leave the bike behind the counter and I'll call up a patrol car right away."

Jamie gave a sigh of relief.

WPC Wilson and PC Cox drove through the estate with Jamie in the back of their patrol car. "Try the high-rise flats," he suggested. "Maybe Greg's hiding up there."

In the distance lay open marshes and a long dual carriageway which wouldn't give Greg any cover.

"Can you name any of this gang?" asked WPC Wilson.

"Mick Mason was one of them – and he had this mate called Darren. He's got a bloody nose."

"How did he get that?"

"I gave it to him. Wait a minute ..."
They had just passed an alley between some
boarded-up houses. "There's something
going on up there."

"We'll go round," said PC Cox, "and park
just short of the top. If anyone tries to run
we'll have 'em."

Jamie and the two police officers crept
slowly and silently from the patrol car to a
fence. Beside the fence there was a small
footpath that led to the alley.

"Keep out of this," whispered WPC
Wilson. "And leave the action to us. Got it?"

"Got it," said Jamie. Now he could hear
the sound of a struggle and repeated cries
of pain. "Go for it!"

"We're in charge," grinned PC Cox. "Don't you start ordering *us* about."

The police officers ran quietly down the footpath and into the alley.

Jamie heard some shouts of surprise and Greg's voice yelling, "Get them off me. Get them off me now!"

"Don't anyone move," Jamie heard WPC Wilson shout. "We know your families – especially yours, Mick Mason. Anyone who tries to do a runner we'll nick later and then it'll go much worse for you. OK, Jamie – you'd better come and join us."

Sick with worry about Greg, Jamie ran down the footpath and into the alley. Greg was lying on the ground. The others were standing facing the wall while PC Cox frisked them.

"You OK, Greg?" asked Jamie.

"No, I'm not," muttered Greg. "First you take my bike – and then I take this punishment. It's not fair."

"What was that?" asked PC Cox. He didn't trust these boys.

"I can explain," said Jamie hurriedly.

"So can I." Greg got to his feet shakily. "Jamie just made a mistake. It's this lot who stole the bikes and you'll find them stashed away in the old garage. We can show you where."

"What makes you so sure we don't suspect you two as well?" snapped WPC Wilson.

"Yes," said Mick, grabbing his chance as he stood with his face to the fence. "They were nicking bikes like we were and ..." He didn't finish his sentence. He realised that he'd dropped himself in it.

"Thanks for that," said PC Cox with a grin.

"We didn't do it." Greg was horrified. So was Jamie. "We didn't steal any bikes."

"No." PC Cox was still frisking Mick. "I don't think you did – and look what I've found." He held up a key.

"I bet that'll fit the new lock on the door in the garage," said Jamie, relieved. "We had to break it down."

"I didn't hear that," said WPC Wilson. "I reckon we should call up a van and some back-up and we can all go down to the garage in style. How about that, Mick?"

"I didn't do it. I've been stitched up."

"You would say that, wouldn't you?" said WPC Wilson.

Chapter 8
A Really Long Ride

A couple of days later, Jamie and Greg met up on their mountain bikes and went for a cycle ride through the hot summer streets, keeping well away from the garage and the flats.

Mick had signed a statement confessing to stealing the bikes and had also grassed his mates, including Bernie. As a result, Jamie and Greg had not only been completely cleared but the police had told them they had acted with great bravery.

"I keep feeling like I dropped you in it, Greg," said Jamie.

"You did. But it couldn't be helped. Have you got a new padlock yet?"

"You bet I have."

"Let's stop and get a drink then."

When they came out of the shop, the two mountain bikes were still safely padlocked to the lamp post.

"Let's go for a really long ride," suggested Jamie. "Right out in the country."

"Sounds a good idea," replied Greg. "I need to get Mick and his mates right out of my head."

Greg's a mate now, thought Jamie. He paused. Odd thing is, if I hadn't lost my bike, I'd never have met him. So something came out of all that mess-up.

"Let's move," said Jamie. "Let's *really* go for it."

He began to pedal as fast as he could and Greg could only just keep up with him. But then Jamie had had plenty of training.

Barrington Stoke would like to thank all its readers for commenting on the manuscript before publication and in particular:

Connor Chilcott
Stewart Corbett
Fiona McNaught
James McNaught
Anne Wilson
Tracy Young

Barrington Stoke Club

Would you like to become a member of our club? Children who write to us with their views become members of our club and special advisors to the company. They also have the chance to act as editors on future manuscripts. Contact us at the address or website below – we'd love to hear from you!

Barrington Stoke, 10 Belford Terrace, Edinburgh EH4 3DQ
Tel: 0131 315 4933 Fax: 0131 315 4934
E-mail: barringtonstoke@cs.com
Website: www.barringtonstoke.co.uk

If you loved this story, why don't you read ..

Tod in Biker City

by Anthony Masters

Could you survive in a world that had become a total desert? A world where you had to fight for water? Tod's father finds a source of water but his discovery puts the whole family in great danger and it's up to Tod to save them.

You can order this book directly from:
Macmillan Distribution Ltd, Brunel Road, Houndmills,
Basingstoke, Hampshire RG21 6XS   Tel: 01256 302699